D0772600

Dear Parent:
Your child's love of reading starts here!

Every child learns to read in a different way and at his or her own speed. Some go back and forth between reading levels and read favorite books again and again. Others read through each level in order. You can help your young reader improve and become more confident by encouraging his or her own interests and abilities. From books your child reads with you to the first books he or she reads alone, there are I Can Read Books for every stage of reading:

SHARED READING
Basic language, word repetition, and whimsical illustrations, ideal for sharing with your emergent reader

BEGINNING READING
Short sentences, familiar words, and simple concepts for children eager to read on their own

READING WITH HELP
Engaging stories, longer sentences, and language play for developing readers

READING ALONE
Complex plots, challenging vocabulary, and high-interest topics for the independent reader

I Can Read Books have introduced children to the joy of reading since 1957. Featuring award-winning authors and illustrators and a fabulous cast of beloved characters, I Can Read Books set the standard for beginning readers.

A lifetime of discovery begins with the magical words **"I Can Read!"**

Visit www.icanread.com for information
on enriching your child's reading experience.

Visit www.zonderkidz.com/icanread for more faith-based
I Can Read! titles from Zonderkidz.

ZONDERKIDZ

I Can Read Fiona Plays Soccer
Copyright © 2023 by Zondervan
Illustrations: © 2023 by Zondervan

An **I Can Read Book**

Requests for information should be
addressed to:
Zonderkidz, 3900 *Sparks Drive SE*,
Grand Rapids, Michigan 49546

Softcover ISBN 978-0-310-75806-8
Hardcover ISBN 978-0-310-75892-1
Ebook ISBN 978-0-310-76197-6

Library of Congress Cataloging-in-Publication Data

Names: Cowdrey, Richard, illustrator. | Wu, Donald, illustrator.
Title: Fiona plays soccer / New York Times bestselling illustrator
      Richard Cowdrey with Donald Wu.
Description: Grand Rapids, Michigan : Zonderkidz, [2023] | Series: I can
      read standards | Audience: Ages 4-8. | Summary: Fiona the hippo and her
      friends find a soccer ball and decide to play a game.
Identifiers: LCCN 2022013228 (print) | LCCN 2022013229 (ebook) | ISBN
      9780310758068 (paperback) | ISBN 9780310758921 (hardcover) | ISBN
      9780310761976 (ebook)
Subjects: CYAC: Soccer—Fiction. | Fiona (Hippopotamus), 2017—Fiction. |
      Hippopotamus—Fiction. | Zoo animals—Fiction. | BISAC: JUVENILE FICTION
      / Animals / Zoos | JUVENILE FICTION / Sports & Recreation / Soccer |
      LCGFT: Animal fiction. | Picture books.
Classification: LCC PZ7.1.C685 Fi 2022 (print) | LCC PZ7.1.C685 (ebook) |
      DDC [E]—dc23
LC record available at https://lccn.loc.gov/2022013228
LC ebook record available at https://lccn.loc.gov/2022013229

Art direction and design: Diane Mielke
Content Contributor: Barbara Herndon

I Can Read® and I Can Read Book® are trademarks of HarperCollins Publishers.

Printed in United States of America

23 24 25 26 27 /LB/ 15 14 13 12 11 10 9 8 7 6 5 4 3 2 1

ZONDERkidz 1 BEGINNING READING I Can Read!

Fiona Plays Soccer

New York Times Bestselling Illustrator
Richard Cowdrey
and Donald Wu

ZONDERkidz

It was a sunny day at the zoo.

Fiona was taking a walk
with Flamingo.

Fiona saw something!

It was black and white.

"What is this?" asked Fiona.

Fiona pushed her nose
into a big, green bush.
Flamingo peeked
into the bush too.

Out popped a
black and white ball!
"It is a soccer ball!

Do you want to play,
Flamingo?"
asked Fiona.

"Yes," said Flamingo.

"Soccer balls are for kicking."

Flamingo kicked the ball.

10

The soccer ball went up.
It went up, up, up
into a tree!

"Help!" called Fiona.

"Our soccer ball is in a tree."

Just then the monkeys swung by.
"We will get your ball, Fiona.
Then may we play?"
asked the monkeys.

"Yes!" said Fiona.

The monkeys pushed the ball

out of the tree.

The ball bounce, bounce,
bounced.
It bounced right into
the seal's pond.

"Help!" called Fiona.
"Our soccer ball is in
the seal's pond!"

Just then, Seal's head
popped out of the water.
The ball was on Seal's nose!

17

"Here is your ball, Fiona,"
said Seal.

"May I play too?"

"Yes!" said Fiona.
Seal bounced the ball
out of the pond.

MEERKATS

It rolled and rolled
and rolled.
The ball rolled right into
a meerkat hole.

21

"Help!" called Fiona.
"Our soccer ball is in
a meerkat hole."

The meerkats came out
of their holes.
They wanted to play
soccer too.

Fiona had a good idea.
The animals could all play
soccer together.

"Let's go to the big, green
grass park.
We can all play with the
soccer ball," she said.

The meerkats carried the ball.

Flamingo and Fiona followed.

The monkeys and Seal
followed too.

"Let's play soccer!" said Fiona.

"We can do this together."

The soccer ball was kicked.

The soccer ball was bounced.

The soccer ball was rolled.

Fiona had a fun day
playing soccer
with her friends.

"Let's play again tomorrow,"
called Fiona, as she walked
home kicking and bouncing
her ball.